For our Westminster
Friends ~

Paul Mulberry

2008

COUNTING SHEEP
DOESN'T MAKE ME SLEEP

BY PAUL E. WEATHINGTON

JuneKat Books

Atlanta, Georgia

Published by
JuneKat Books, LLC
191 Peachtree Street NE, Suite 3900
Atlanta, Georgia 30303

ISBN: 978-1-60585-575-2 (HC)

Library of Congress Control Number: 2008901189

Printed in Canada

Contact Information

For ordering information, upcoming books
and information on our company, please visit us on the web at:

www.JuneKatBooks.com

Or contact us by mail at:

JuneKat Books, LLC
191 Peachtree Street NE, Suite 3900
Atlanta, Ga. 30303
Telephone: 404-524-1600 • Fax: 404-524-1610

4/08
E
Wea
SGL 38171
$15.95

To Katherine and Paul Jr. for letting me read all those books to you

and inspiring me to write better ones.

To the first 5 kids, Ryan, Austin, Carter, Shannon and Michael

for all the bad singing you tolerated as I rocked you to sleep.

To my late father, Grover Milford, for your sense of humor and for not naming me Junior.

To my mother Elizabeth for your kind heart and lofty goals.

To my brother Neil for your patience and for looking after mom.

To my nephew and niece, Adam and Emily, and their parents, Lucy and Tracy Batchelor,

for reading my books with your Boston accents.

To all the members of The Weathington Firm for helping me keep my day job.

And to my loving wife, Molly, for all you do and have done, and for tucking me in at night.

Being awake is so much fun
it's hard to go to sleep
when the day is done.

Our parents try all sorts of tricks;

singing songs, reading books . . .

but the results are mixed.

So last night to get me to sleep,
mom suggested that I count the sheep.

Why count sheep?
Where'd that come from?
Counting cute furry lambs
seemed so dumb!

But I thought,
what the heck,
I'll give it a try.
I'll picture me some sheep
in my mind's eye.

So as I tried to count sheep
with my eyes closed tight,
I saw something else
and it was quite a sight.

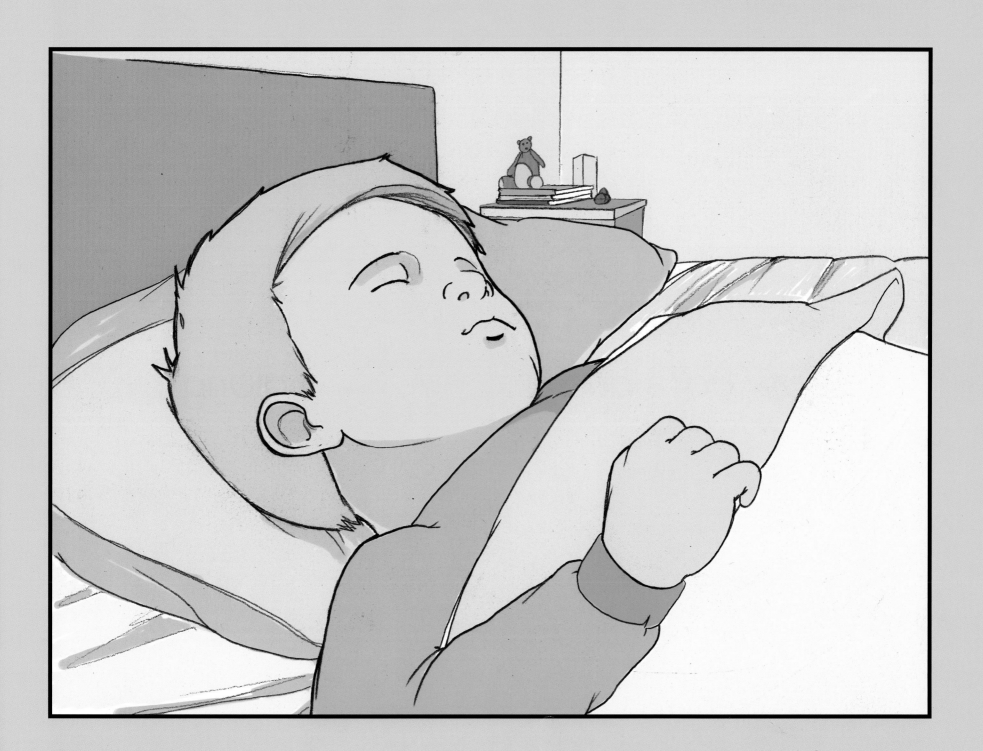

I saw cats and dogs getting along . . .

and boys and girls singing the same song.

I saw sunny days without end,
and just enough rain
for the grass to mend!

I saw my favorite food
and things to drink,
and beautiful art work
in all colors of ink.

I saw all my favorite teams
on the winning side . . .

and a handsome prince
kissing his beautiful bride.

I saw Christmas trees
with tons of toys underneath . . .

and mom kissing dad
under the mistletoe wreath.

So, with my eyes shut tight
and sleeping real sound,
I saw all my favorite things,
but no sheep to be found!

I woke about 10
and *jumped* from the bed . . .
a great night's sleep,
but I was scratching my head.

I slept like a baby
but never saw any sheep.
What a clever little trick
to get me to sleep.

Now I have sweet dreams every night
running through my head,
but I still haven't seen any sheep
jumping over my bed.

About the Author

Mr. Weathington grew up in Carrollton, Georgia. He is an attorney practicing in Atlanta, Georgia who has authored over a dozen children's books. "Counting Sheep Doesn't Make Me Sleep" is his second formal publication. Mr. Weathington is the father of seven children ranging in age from 4 to 22. Hence, he has plenty of material for his books.

About the Illustrator

Jonathan Bass was born in Chapel Hill, North Carolina in 1981. A graduate of the Savannah College of Art and Design in 2007, he currently works as a freelance artist and illustrator in Atlanta, Georgia.

Other books by Mr. Weathington

Titles currently available

Bed Bugs Don't Bite

～

Counting Sheep Doesn't Make Me Sleep

– Upcoming releases –

Where is the Man On the Moon (March 2008)

～

Lightning Shoes (April 2008)

～

Ish, Ish, Almost Made a Fish!

～

Quick, Quick, I've Got a Cowlick!

Contact Information

For ordering information, upcoming books
and information on our company, please visit us on the web at:

www.JuneKatBooks.com

Or contact us by mail at:

JuneKat Books, LLC

191 Peachtree Street NE, Suite 3900

Atlanta, Ga. 30303

Telephone: 404-524-1600 • Fax: 404-524-1610